Illustrated by
Steve Haskamp

An Aesop Fable
adapted by
Margery Cuyler

Roadsigns

A Harey race
with a tortoise

WINSLOW PRESS

DELRAY BEACH, FLORIDA • NEW YORK

Cuyler, Margery.
Road signs / written by Margery Cuyler ; illustrated by Steve Haskamp.
First Edition
p.   cm.
Summary: Tortoise and Hare race along a road filled with traffic signs
while the other animals cheer them on.
ISBN 1-890817-23-6
[1. Traffic signs and signals-Fiction. 2. Racing-Fiction. 3. Tortoises-Fiction. 4. Hares-Fiction. 5. Animals-Fiction.]
I. Haskamp, Steve, ill. II. Title.
PZ7+
[E]-dc21
99-462278

All rights reserved
Library of Congress catalog card number: 99-462278
Creative Designer: Bretton Clark
Designed by Billy Kelly
Editor: Margery Cuyler
Letter Art by Jessica Wolk-Stanley
Printed in Belgium

This book has a trade reinforced binding.

For games, links and more, visit our interactive Web site:
www.winslowpress.com

To Diane, Brett and Billy
—M.C.

For my family
—S.H.

One windy spring day, Hare challenged Tortoise to a race. Hare was sure that he would win, but would he?

REST ROOMS

Some signs in this book:

CURVE

DETOUR AHEAD

YIELD

DETOUR →

SLOW

SLOW DOWN

ROAD CONSTRUCTION 1000 FT

BRIDGE CLOSED

BLASTING ZONE 1000 FT

(rock being dynamited ahead)

PASS WITH CARE

EXIT

TUNNEL

CAUTION CHILDREN AT PLAY

END CONSTRUCTION

NO PARKING

FALLING ROCK

DANGER

SLIPPERY WHEN WET

(road is slippery when it rains)

ONE WAY →

PAVEMENT ENDS

NO PASSING IN TUNNEL

R R

FLOOD AREA

DO NOT STOP ON TRACKS

ROAD CLOSED AHEAD

REST AREA ↗

ROAD MACHINERY AHEAD

KEEP LEFT

BUMP

STEEP HILL

DIP

10 M.P.H.

SCHOOL ZONE AHEAD

SOFT SHOULDER

(no pavement on side of road)

STOP

TURN LIGHTS ON

SCHOOL BUS STOP